Sit Sit

Written by Sarah Rice

Illustrated by Anna Kazimi

Collins

T0364449

sit

sit

3

tap

4

tap

5

a tin

tip tip

a pan

pat pat

tap tap

sip sip

tap tap

sit sit

14

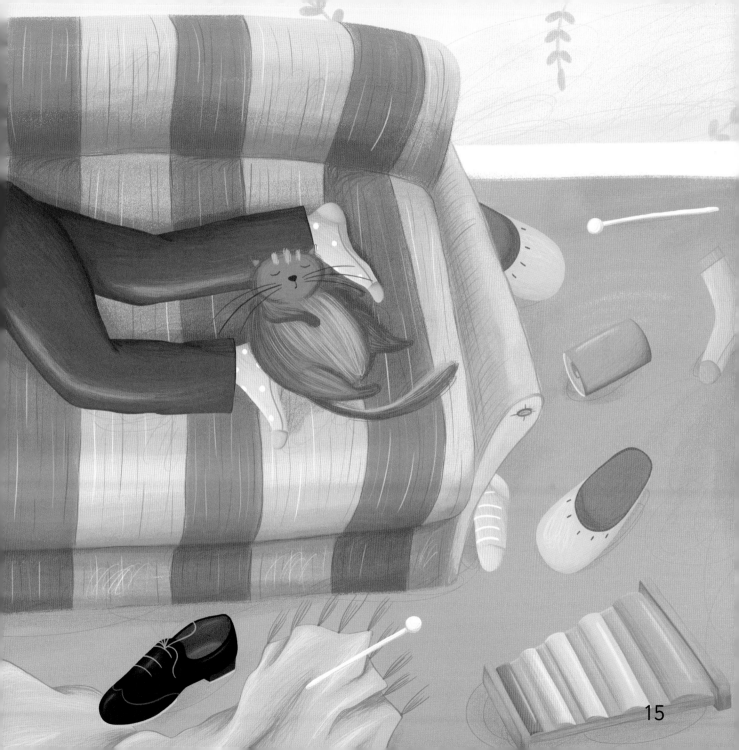

After reading

Letters and Sounds: Phase 2

Word count: 20

Focus phonemes: /s/ /a/ /t/ /p/ /i/ /n/

Common exception word: a

Curriculum links: Expressive arts and design: Exploring and using media and materials ... make music

Early learning goals: Reading: use phonic knowledge to decode regular words and read them aloud accurately, demonstrate understanding when talking with others about what they have read

Developing fluency

- Your child may enjoy hearing you read the book.
- You may wish to take turns to read a page.

Phonic practice

- Say the word **sip** on page 11. Ask your child if they can sound out each of the letter sounds in the word **sip** s/i/p and then blend them.
- Now ask them to do the same with the following words:

  tap   sit   pan

- Look at the "I spy sounds" pages (14–15) together. How many words can your child point out that contain the /s/ sound? (e.g. *sleeping, scarf, shoe, sandwich, sock, sandal*)

Extending vocabulary

- Look at the pictures together.
- Ask your child to tell you the story, in their own words.
- Can they think of different words for the sound noises? (e.g. *bang, clip clop*)